Ivor Jones trained as a highway engineer before joining Britannia Royal Naval College, Dartmouth on a flying course. After the Navy, he worked as a photographer before retiring to Somerset. Writing interests included submissions to 'Week Ending', 'News Huddlines', and local newspapers. He has also produced original material for a group of visually-impaired actors.

To my daughters, Victoria and Rebecca, for whom the original 'Wind Fairy' bedtime stories came about. They can certainly vouch for the soporific effect of my efforts – having to wake me up on numerous occasions!

To Bethany

With best wishes

from [signature]

Ivor Jones

THE SPIRIT WITHIN THE WIND

Original artwork by Thelma Frost

AUSTIN MACAULEY
PUBLISHERS LTD.

Original artwork by Thelma Frost

A CIP catalogue record for this title is available from the British Library.

ISBN 9781786121400 (Paperback)
ISBN 9781786121417 (Hardback)
ISBN 9781786121424 (E-Book)

www.austinmacauley.com

First Published (2016)
Austin Macauley Publishers Ltd.
25 Canada Square
Canary Wharf
London
E14 5LQ

Contents

The Spirit Within the Wind

One day in the sky,
Said the old Weather Clerk,
"Today, Wind Spirit,
You must blow until dark."

"Remember it's summer –
You must take it easy.
So nothing much more
Than a little bit breezy."

And so the Wind Spirit
Then went on his way
Knowing how he should
Behave for that day.

He wafted around
For a couple of hours
Gently moving the clouds,
The trees and the flowers.

But soon he thought this
Was so awfully tame
Preferring instead
To play a fun game.

So although it was meant
As a warm summer's day
He was soon looking out
For some tricks he might play.

He looked all about him
And saw a windmill
Perched close to the top
Of Much Pottering Hill...

Ted the Miller

The windmill's big sails
Were going round and round
With that friendly familiar
'Pa-don-ka' sound.

Inside, Ted the miller
Was working away,
For he had to produce
Lots of flour that day.

He went to the door
And looked up at the sky
Saying, "I'll get plenty done
Today, if I try."

The Wind Spirit found himself
Wanting to know
Precisely how fast
Those old sails would go!

And so down he flew
To take a close look
At the miller
And all the trouble he took,

To ensure he was able
To make enough flour
And see how many sacks
He would fill in an hour.

"Tee hee," thought the Wind Spirit,
"This could be fun –
At this gentle speed,
He might fill only one."

"With a little more puff
And a bit more again,
The miller could easily
Fill eight or ten!"

"Then again, if I want
To be ever so naughty
And I blow really hard
He might do nearer forty!"

So he blew a bit harder
On Pottering Hill
And harder again
Then a bit harder still.

Now the miller, concerned
At the quickening sails' pace
Would have really preferred
They were going at a snail's pace.

But by now, those sails
Were turning so fast
The miller was hoping
This wind would not last.

Wind Spirit thought, "Whoops,
That is just a bit strong.
It's a good job I can't
Keep this up very long!"

So he stopped, and the sails
Soon lost all their power.
Just in time, as the miller
All covered in flour

And very concerned
At the sails going so fast
Realised they had started
To slow down – at last.

"And not before time,"
He heard himself say,
"I think that I've milled
Quite enough for today."

Peggy Pegg's Laundry

Wind Spirit, on seeing
What he had just done
Thought, "Naughty or not –
That really was fun!"

And soon, having left
The old mill far behind
Was wondering what
Other mischief he'd find.

And surely he didn't have
Too far to go
When, whom should he spot
On the ground far below?

The laundry lady –
Peggy Pegg was her name –
Fresh, crisp and clean washing
Was her claim to fame.

She, too, came out
And looked up at the sky
Saying, "What a nice day
For my laundry to dry."

Then she went back inside
And was happily humming
Not knowing the mischievous
Wind Spirit was coming.

And soon she had filled
Each and every clothes line
For she knew they'd soon dry
If the weather stayed fine.

Back inside she then went
Again, happily singing
Unaware of the problems
Wind Spirit was bringing.

And so he flew down
For a much better view
Where he gleefully thought
Of the things he could do.

So he started to blow,
Very gently at first,
Then harder, 'til Mrs Pegg
Fearing the worst

Looked out to see
What the laundry was doing
And realised that something
Unusual was brewing.

Those things she had lovingly
Pegged out to dry
Were blowing out straight
In that wind rushing by.

Then, as the strong wind
Gusted round even stronger
Those pegs were unable
To hold any longer.

And, piece after piece,
The clean laundry broke free
Some blown into bushes,
Yet more up a tree.

With pants in the pansies,
Six socks and a shirt,
One minute so clean,
The next, covered in dirt.

Mrs Pegg was not pleased
When she saw what was done
Said, "I hope this is not
Someone's idea of fun.

And now that I have
To wash this lot again,
I really do hope
It's not going to rain."

Farmer Jack Barleycorn

By now our Wind Spirit
Had gone on his way
Thinking of how many more
Tricks he might play.

Then farmer Jack Barleycorn
Hove into view.
He had stopped to shake out
A big stone from his shoe.

And that very morning
He'd bought a new hat
Which was brown, quite round
And incredibly flat.

Wind Spirit puffed lightly
And, taking some care,
Lifted this new hat
High into the air.

The poor farmer grabbed
At the hat he'd just bought,
But try as he might
The hat wouldn't be caught!

Those old farmer's legs
Had to try running fast
And he finally caught up
With his new hat – at last.

"I've got you!" he cried.
As he lunged for the brim,
Wind Spirit blew gently
And snatched it from him.

And it rolled like a wheel
On its firm flat edge
'Til it stuck itself fast
In a thorny old hedge.

Now, by pushing and tugging
Jack rescued his hat,
But it never would look
Quite the same after that.

The state of this new hat
He did not find funny.
Because old Farmer Jack
Hated parting with money.

Its colour, when bought,
Was a smart rustic brown.
It was now muddy grey
With a dent in the crown!

The broad brim was buckled,
The inside was torn.
Who'd ever have thought
It had hardly been worn?

So now with this 'new' hat
Jammed firm on his head,
He wished he had stuck
With his old one instead

Although he was pleased
To have got his hat back,
Farmer Jack was now far
From his intended track.

So he mumbled and stumbled
His way to the gate.
Then when he had reached it
Was not so irate.

"If I'd wanted an old hat
To wear in a gale,
I'd have found one last week
In our church jumble sale!"

And he muttered and frowned
As he went on his way
Then resolved not to let
This thing spoil his day!

The Boy on a Raft

Having had so much fun
With the farmer's new hat
The Wind Spirit wondered,
"How do I follow that?

"I know what I'll do;
I'll go down to the sea,
For there I might find
More to interest me!"

So up and away
The Wind Spirit flew
And lo, the blue sea
Came into his view

Then he spotted a boy
On an inflatable raft,
"Goodness me," thought the Wind Spirit,
"He must be daft!"

"He is out much too far
On so windy a day
And could be in real danger
Of drifting away."

So gently he blew him
Straight back to the land
Where the boy, feeling lucky,
Jumped onto the sand.

His Dad was so cross
And pulled him up the beach.
"You must never again
Go so far from my reach!

"It's only a sunbed
Not a sailing raft, Billy.
I'll take it away
If you're going to be silly!

"It's a good job the wind
Blew you back to the shore –
Now, let's go and find
Some rock pools to explore."

The Two Jolly Sailors

Not far off the coast
Sailed a tiny red boat.
With but two men on board
It just managed to float.

So around the red boat
The Wind Spirit blew
'Til the waves were so large
The craft vanished from view!

When up bobbed the boat,
The crew were all wet.
"My, my," laughed the skipper,
"That's our biggest wave yet!"

"So let's find another,"
Said he, feeling brave,
"We're wearing our lifejackets,
Now, where's that next wave?"

The more the wind blew,
Our sailors got wetter.
They liked a rough sea
So it couldn't be better!

They were having such fun
On their afternoon out,
Shouting 'Lee-ho' and 'Gybe-ho',
And 'Ready-about!'.

The Family on the Beach

Just far enough up
From high tide's normal reach
A family of four
Was ensconced on the beach.

"Oh, what a nice place,"
Said the mum to the dad.
"Yes, yes, we agree!"
Chorused Suzie and Brad.

As they started their picnic
At Smugglers' Bay
The Wind Spirit blew
Their striped wind-break away!

Their lunch was so special
And beautifully planned
But the cucumber sandwiches
All tasted of sand!

And Mummy's best fairy-cakes
Looking so pretty
Had all ended up
Tasting salty and gritty.

It looked like the wind
Might drive them away.
Or should they stay there
For the rest of the day?

But by now that wind
Was no more than a breeze.
And soon Brad was digging
Right up to his knees!

While Suzie played ball
With her Mum and her Dad.
Who cares what the wind does
When fun's to be had?

Back to the Town

As he headed back inland,
The Wind Spirit knew
In a town he might find
Lots more mischief to do!

So, picking up some speed
Very soon he could see
Small houses, tall buildings
And an occasional tree.

But most of all, people
Still charging about –
Some travelling in
Others trying to get out.

There were buses and cars
And some lorries as well
Making terrible noise
But an even worse smell.

It didn't take too much
To know what was wrong.
He would have to blow hard
To get rid of that pong!

With a jolly good puff
And a powerful blow
The Wind Spirit cleared
That whole pong in one go!

It was all very nice
To get rid of the smell,
But he brought down some trees
And a chimney as well!

29

The Town Hall Flag

The standard hung limply
Outside the Town Hall
When, out of the blue
It was hit by a squall.

In the strengthening breeze
The flag started to flap.
Soon the cleats and the halyards
Began to tap-tap.

As the wind gathered pace
That old flag started tearing.
A new one would have to be
Much more hardwearing.

The Wind Spirit laughed.
How he chuckled with glee.
For who was responsible?
Of course – it was he!

The Mayor and Mayoress
Inspected the flag.
She sighed, "It now looks
Like a tattered old rag."

And Brian the Mayor
Looked somewhat perplexed
For he had to decide
What he'd have to do next!

He looked at the flagstaff
And said with a frown,
"That thing is quite rotten –
It'll have to come down."

"We all love our town
And its name, 'Nether Snoring'
But the townsfolk complain
That it's just a bit boring."

"We must change its image",
Said Brian's wife, Wendy,
"Let's have a new flag –
That will make it more trendy".

It didn't take long
Once the idea was known.
It had been many years
Since a new flag was flown.

"We'll ask all the children
And offer a prize
For the best flag design
Seen through young people's eyes."

The youngsters decided.
Their theme for the flag
Should be bright wavy lines
And the head of a stag.

The Mayor had a thought,
"New flag, needs a new pole,"
So he sent out five men
To start digging a hole.

To the Town Square they went
There to fence off some ground.
Soon, two men started digging
While the others stood round!

The hole was so neat
And the bottom was clean,
Then they measured it
Using a laser machine.

The foreman said,
"Right lads, that's OK by me."
So they all disappeared
For a nice cup of tea!

Next day they returned
With the gleaming new pole
And fixed it with sand and cement
Down the hole.

And there the flag flies
'Til the windiest day
When it's soon taken down
And put carefully away!

Mikey and His Kite

As for young Mikey:
Out flying his new kite
Soon found it was only
The string he held tight!

That powerful gust
Had broken the string
And Mikey, poor lad,
Had felt it go 'ping'.

To fly a big kite
Was his dream that came true
And something he'd wanted
For ages to do!

This kite was a gift
From the previous day
Thanks to great-uncle Cecil
And great-auntie May.

Alas, he went home
Sad to say, empty-handed
For he had not a clue
Where his new toy had landed.

"But hang on," he thought,
"Things could still turn out right,
Because I wrote my name
And address on my kite!

My great-uncle Cecil
Advised me to do it
So that may well not be
The last time I flew it!"

Mister MacBain

Meanwhile, out on the street
Was a Mr MacBain
Who was sure as could be
It was going to rain

So he'd bought an umbrella
In case the rain fell
But he had not allowed
For a strong wind as well!

And he knew from experience,
No shadow of doubt,
That a very strong gust
Would blow it inside out.

With no rain, only wind
Forecast for that day
He took his new brolly
And packed it away.

But wait – if the forecaster
Had got it all wrong,
Then Angus MacBain
Had been right all along.

So he unpacked the brolly again
In a hurry.
Whatever the weather does –
No need to worry.

Tracey and Rupert's Wedding

Now, down at the church
Where Wind Spirit was heading,
Tracey and Rupert
Emerged from their wedding.

Under the bride's gown
In comfort and freedom,
She wore her white wellies
In case she might need 'em.

While the groom looked
So dapper and ever so smart.
Small wonder he'd stolen
His fair lady's heart

The crowd threw confetti
At bridegroom and bride
But covered the photographer
Waiting outside!

The cameraman said,
"Just one more time, but please –
Don't throw any more stuff
Until I say 'cheese'.

"The wind took the last lot
Which missed them by miles.
Now I shan't take your photos
Until I get smiles!

"So please, look this way –
Hurry up – *Do you mind?*
Don't worry about
What they're doing behind."

"I don't think that lady
Has heard what I said -
I've just taken a snap
Of the back of her head!

I warn you, I'll get
Very cross in a minute
And do just a small group
With none of you in it!"

"Now, now," said the Vicar
Who'd come to the door,
"Let us calmly arrange
Just a few photos more.

"Remember that this
Is a happy event.
Please don't misconstrue
What the photographer meant."

Then everyone smiled
And held the right poses
Except two small boys
Who stood picking their noses.

"So," spluttered the Vicar,
Who'd spotted the pair,
"You just can't take little…tinkers
Like that anywhere!

"It's the parents I blame
For the way they behave.
Ah well, must crack on –
Plenty more souls to save!"

The News Vendor

"Read all about it,"
The street vendor cried
With a tall stack of newspapers
Piled up outside.

Then, puff came the wind
At the pile so neat
And into the air
Flew sheet after sheet.

"Oh heavens, oh dear,"
Said the man in distress,
"Those papers will make
One heck of a mess!"

The news vendor grabbed
All the copies he could.
But despite all his efforts,
Things didn't look good.

In fact, most untidy,
Of that, there's no doubt,
With dozens of papers
All scattered about.

Then, after securing
The rest of the stack
The poor man eventually
Got them all back!

"Phew, that was lucky,"
He sighed, "What a caper."
As he wearily picked up
The last piece of paper.

Jim the Cyclist

Up Mucklebury Hill,
A cyclist named Jim
Went racing along
With the wind behind him.

He got to the top
And then onto the flat,
Thinking, "No wind assistance
Was ever like that!"

He mused to himself
"What a wonderful wheeze,
To be driven uphill
By the strength of the breeze.

But there's no guarantee
That this wind's going to last
And could my old bike
Cope with going so fast?"

Then, thinking aloud,
"Well, perhaps on reflection,
T'would be awfully hard work
In the opposite direction!"

But Jim was still pleased
As he pedalled away.
And wished it would help him
Like that every day.

The Camp Site

A popular place
Is Furrowhayes Farm,
Well known for its old
Rustic beauty and charm

But where you would once
See a sheep or a cow
Everything's changed –
It's a camping site now.

And so people come
From near and far
Some come on their bikes
But mostly by car.

For weeks and weeks
They've made their plans
To bring their tents
And caravans.

When tenters have finished
With guy ropes and pegs
They sit round their campfires
Eating bacon and eggs.

The caravanners have simply
To put out their awning
Then they can relax
'Til they wake up next morning.

That day's weather forecast
Said 'Sunny and warm',
But dark clouds approaching
Portended a storm

So back to their tents
For a minute or two –
False alarm. Clouds are gone
And the sky's back to blue.

With horses to ride
And big trees to climb
Those children all have
Such a wonderful time.

Those neddies know all
The familiar tracks
And don't seem to mind
Whom they have on their backs.

And as for the wind
It just left them alone
They'd surely have so much
More fun on their own

Adventures so daring
With friendships so dear.
Good times they'll remember
For many a year.

The Circus Comes to Town

There's a circus in town
And in the Big Top
There'd be no show tonight
If that wind doesn't stop.

The Ringmaster summoned
The whole cast and said,
"If it's too windy later,
We can't go ahead.

I'm sorry, but acts
Like the flying trapeze
Cannot perform safely
In more than a breeze."

Then up spoke a clown
A tall fellow called Stan,
"We'll have to come up
With a different plan.

The children all laugh
At my baggy clown suits
And the way that I juggle
In those big yellow boots.

They all think that it's
Just the funniest thing
When my car falls to bits
As I drive 'round the ring

With my big red nose
And funny white face,
The sound of their laughter
Will fill the whole place.

If we cancel, our public
Will feel they're forsaken
And we'll have to refund
All the ticket-money we've taken!

Then, if we return
All the money we've made –
Remember, my friends,
That no-one gets paid!"

"But wait; now it seems
Those strong gusts have all gone –
So it looks like, tonight
Our show will go on!"

"Hurrah," yelled the cast
At this wonderful news
So the high-wire walker
Rushed off for her shoes!

The human projectile
Was not convinced yet
For he had to be sure
That he'd land in the net!

Unlike a performance
Performed recently,
When he'd had to climb down
From the top of a tree!

On a previous tour
The Doctor had said,
"With a little less luck,
You'd have broken your head!"

So deep down inside
This cannonball knew
That he'd have to find something
Less dangerous to do!

The Hairdressing Salon

At the hairdressing salon,
A Monsieur Alphonse
Was working so hard
On an old lady's bonce.

"I'm dancing in Town,
With my husband tonight –
And I want him to think
I'm a bit of all right!"

As she left the salon
On that windiest day
A sudden strong gust
Blew her topknot away.

She rushed back inside
In a state of despair.
"Monsieur Alphonse," she cried
"Just look at my hair!

If my husband sees this
He'll have such a fright.
I'll be the last lady
He takes out tonight!"

Alphonse sighed deeply,
Then said, "Ah, I've got it,
We'll use zis nice wig
And he won't even spot it!"

"Oh, you are such a dear,"
Said she, "You lovely man –
So hurry and fix it on,
Fast as you can."

So pleased and surprised
At what she'd just said,
He tried not to let her words
Go to his head!

And when he had fixed it,
She rose from the chair.
Never before having seen herself
With such beautiful hair

She left the salon
Feeling quite ten feet tall
Believing tonight she'd be
Belle of the Ball.

Dennis the Pilot

Dennis the pilot
Adjusted his goggles
While checking his switches
And dials and toggles,

His glider was ready
To take to the air
Just needing a tow
To get him up there.

Wow! Suddenly he found himself
Winched up so high
As up and away
That glider did fly!

Releasing the cable
He hung in the blue
And soon he decided
What he had to do.

"I must find a thermal
To give me more height."
And in a few moments
He found one, just right.

So he soared like an eagle
Turning and swooping.
Going fast in a dive
Meant plenty of looping.

Such wonderful fun
With green fields far below
But back to the airstrip
Now Dennis must go.

So, circling around
He suddenly saw
The familiar shape
Of the airfield once more.

The Wind Spirit watched
As the glider lost height
And thought "What can I do
To give Dennis a fright?"

On the downwind leg
Things were going as planned
'Til the very last turn
As he came in to land!

A sudden strong gust
Came in from the side
Upsetting the glidepath
That Dennis would glide.

For his final approach
He was now much too high
So he had to correct it.
He knew how to fly!

Pushing stick to the left
And the rudder to right
He neatly sideslipped
To the appropriate height.

And soon he was back again
Down on the ground
A small bounce and he stopped
Home again – safe and sound!

Dennis jumped from the cockpit
And heard himself say,
"That's the best kind of landing –
You just walk away!"

The Park Keeper

Away across town
The park-keeper named Kyle
Had swept all the leaves
Into one great big pile

He'd collected them up
From all over the park
And then as he watched,
The sky went a bit dark.

Then, there, right before
The park-keeper's eyes
Those leaves began moving
And started to rise

"By gum and by gosh,"
Gasped the keeper aloud,
As Kyle's pile held together
Overhead, like a cloud.

"Never mind," reasoned Kyle
As the leaves blew away,
"I'll sweep 'em all up again
Some other day!"

Now all that was left
Was a patch on the ground
With some dust and a twig
Whirling round and around.

Outro

And then, suddenly
The wind lost its puff,
As Wind Spirit realised
"Enough is enough!"

So now our Wind Spirit
Was in a real fix
For he'd have to explain
Why he'd played all those tricks.

But the wise Weather Clerk
Would have known all along
That sometimes on a summer's day
Things can go wrong!

Wind Spirit Comprehension

Intro
1. Who controls the weather?
2. What does the wind do?
3. What is a windmill?
4. Why would a windmill sit near the top of a hill?

Ted the Miller
1. How does a windmill work?
2. Where does flour come from?
3. What is it used for?
4. How can the miller produce more flour?
5. How does he collect it?

Peggy Pegg's Laundry
1. What is a laundry?
2. Who would use one?
3. Why should the weather be so important?
4. What sort of weather is preferable?

Farmer Jack Barleycorn
1. What does a farmer do?
2. What is the meaning of '**hove into view**'?
3. Why might a farmer wear a hat?
4. The hat stuck 'fast' in the hedge. What does 'fast' mean?
5. What is the 'crown' of the hat?
6. Where is the 'brim'?
7. The farmer was 'not so irate' What is 'irate'?
8. What is a Jumble Sale?

The Boy on the Raft
    1   What does 'inflatable' mean?
    2   What does 'daft' mean?
    3   What is a sunbed used for?
    4   Where do you find rock pools?
    5   What are they?
    6   Would anything live in a rock pool?

Two Jolly Sailors
    1   What is another word for a small sailing boat?
    2   What is a lifejacket?
    3   What is it for?
    4   What is a good choice of colour for a lifejacket?
    5   Why?
    6   What do 'Lee ho', 'Gybe ho' and 'Ready about' mean?

The Family on the Beach
    1   What is 'the tide'?
    2   What does 'ensconced' mean?
    3   What is a 'wind break'?
    4   What does a wind break do?
    5   What is a 'sandwich'?
    6   Were they on a stony beach?

Back to the Town
    1   Why do buses, cars and lorries make noise?
    2   What makes them smell?
    3   What is a 'chimney'?
    4   How could the wind bring one down?

The Town Hall Flag
    1   What is a 'standard'?
    2   What is a 'squall'?
    3   Where else would you also find cleats and halyards?
    4   What does a 'Mayor' do?
    5   What is a 'stag'?

6   Why use sand and cement down the hole?

7   When do they usually take down the flag?

Mikey and his Kite
1   What is a 'kite' in this case?

2   Is there a different sort of kite?

3   How might Mikey be able to get his kite back?

Mister MacBain
1   How did he hope to stay dry if it rained?

2   From which country might he have come?

Tracey and Rupert's Wedding
1   What are a bride and groom?

2   What are 'wellies'?

3   Are they normal wear at weddings?

4   What does 'dapper' mean?

5   What is confetti?

6   How is it used?

7   Why would a photographer start talking about 'cheese'?

8   What is the meaning of 'misconstrue'?

The News Vendor
1   What does a 'vendor' do?

2   What happened to his newspapers?

Jim the Cyclist
1   What was unusual about Jim's ride uphill?

2   Was wind assistance helpful there?

3   What does 'cope' mean?

The Camp Site
1   What does 'rustic' mean?

2   What is an 'awning'?

3   Where does an awning go?

4   What does 'portended' mean?
5   Do the horses know the local hacking tracks?

The Circus Comes to Town
1   What is a 'circus'?
2   Why is the 'Big Top' so called?
3   Who is the 'Ringmaster'?
4   What is a 'trapeze'?
5   Why does a circus clown look so different?
6   What is the meaning of 'refund'?
7   Are shoes important to a high-wire walker?
8   What is a 'human projectile'?
9   Why was he so worried?
10   Was he likely soon to change his job?

The Hairdressing Salon
1   From which country might Monsieur Alphonse have come?
2   What is another, more polite word for 'bonce'?
3   Where should the lady's 'topknot' normally be?
4   How did Monsieur Alphonse solve the problem?

Dennis the Pilot
1   What does a pilot do?
2   What are 'goggles'?
3   What is different about a glider from other aircraft?
4   Why is a 'thermal' so useful?
5   Is 'downwind' important?
6   What are the 'stick' and 'rudder'?

The Park Keeper
1   What would Kyle have used to sweep up the leaves?
2   What does a Park Keeper do?

Outro
1   What is the wind's 'puff'?
2   Are weather forecasts always right?